# Secret
# Words
# V

Vegetarian Alcoholic Press
as read by Freddy La Force
and selected by majority rule

# BUST

## Air Quality

The pollen at this time of year
is unforgivingly thick,
and spore sacs bust with fecundity.

Our eyes are red and watery;
the river and your nose both run.

But the dust is worth this sun
that has come back to us

after too much frozen night

It is a joy to thaw with you,
to muck about in the sluices.

I would sneeze with you for eons.

**–Lily Lalios**

In the days of yore, it was believed that disquiet of the mind was only treatable by repanation, the drilling of a hole into the skull. Humankind has since learned that it is, in fact, an overstimulation of the nerves which causes such maladies. Boozy libations, spicy foods, and chronic masturbation are all culprits in the deterioration of the spirit.

Fortunately, Dr. Wilber T. Gilbenworm has devised a lifestyle regimen to sooth the jangled soul! This regimen consists of waking promptly at 5:00 AM for two hours of lifting barbells and tossing a medicine ball. From 7:00 until noon, time is spent contemplating the Bible. The midday meal of nutritious grain paste will keep the mind and body fit throughout the remainder of the day.

A key component of this regimen is the frequent imbibement of Dr. W.T. Gilbenworm's All-Purpose Health Tonic. Now, for the first time, Dr. W.T. Gilbenworm's All-Purpose Health Tonic is available to the common public. Dr. W.T. Gilbenworm's All-Purpose Health Tonic is guaranteed to cure the following ailments:

- Bilious fever
- Consumption
- Busted duodenum
- Cobbler's complaint
- Gravedigger's delight
- The quakes
- St. Victoria's nightmare
- Lobe of Liverpool
- Grey eyebrows (but the rest of hair isn't grey)
- One-pinkey-is-longer-than-the-
- other disease
- The grumps
- The chumps
- Greek flu
- The bumps

- Bad vibes
- Vice-President's bones
- Dutch Elm disease
- Belgian Poplar syndrome
- "Mister Potato" head
- Too many elbows
- Frostbite
- Town Crier's anguish
- Reverse heartbeat
- Ventriloquist's mishap
- Sinister grime

**– Ben**

## Black Thumb

I don't exactly have a green thumb. When I got my first apartment, living alone for the first time, just like everyone else during the pandemic, I filled that square white box with plants.

At first, I thought they were growing really well. Little did I know that succulents only sprout so tall as a last gasp, a last opportunity to reproduce before falling into the desert-plant-in-a-north-facing-window-in-Wisconsin afterlife.

Oops. There goes $30.

I kept trying, for three years. I really wanted to be the plant girl. After all, I grew up working in my parents' greenhouse. Why did I suddenly kill everything I touched?

It's the third year. I laugh at other people's plant failures on the internet, making myself feel better before I finally close this chapter of my life. It's 6:30 AM. Two by two, I bring the artisan pottery full of perfectly good potting soil and absolutely desiccated tropical leaves to the space behind my garage. As I shake out my creative vessels for dead plants, a cascade of dirt blesses my toes.

It's not like I'm coordinated this early in the morning, creating an above-ground mass grave of various variegations. One pot falls out of the crook in my elbow, hits the garage siding, and breaks. "Aw," I sigh. That was my favorite one. It was a terra cotta bust that looked kind of pretty with dried-up nerve plants coming out of it.

I don't clean up the shards. I shake off my feet and go inside to make coffee.

— **Janae Mancheski**

**THIS ONE SUX**

out of favor, out of FLAVOR
it's a bust
failure to adjust
a conveyor, A purveyor
A FAIR LACK of trust
FEAR NOT, the swift uppercut
Thrust of linguistical lust
should have been a bust
but out of jail
because by luck, your politics
are the right type of corrupt
at night like the light when you look up
ignite a resolve, a dialogue
to understand, you add to your catalogue
you listen, MORE than run on sentences
in your monologues

**– Jacob McElrone**

## FOBO

I used to have FOMO– a fear of missing out. Until, however, I learned about the greater threat of busting out. Like when the "All You Can Drink for $10" special led me to vomit on a cute stranger mid-sentence, and I slipped walking up to the stage, where I never did get to sing karaoke.

The promise of happiness the night contained– it became more of a bad dream, a nightmare. The good time was lost, and I never got to buy that round of shots.

And so from then on, I knew that missing out is better than a bust.

–??

# FLESH

In the flesh
    In the moment
no turning back
    For glory, and prizes
        surprise endings
        get sticky conclusions
        the illusion of safety
        encased meat popsicle
        the robot is Not
        comfortable with touch
        programmed for answers
        but beneath the
        surface is filled
        with questions
        if you can't feel
        anything are you
            really real
        one of those skin deep
            creeps
        dialed in for success
        I can see you
        hear you, taste you
        even smell you (PU)
        But I FEEL NOTHING
        YOU ANDROID FUCK


**– Adam Mckee**

## Women's History Month

   Dig deep enough and you will find me. Exposed, I am vulnerable. To threats, to bets on how quickly, how easily, one can gather me. Caress me. But that's not his intention. He wishes to taste me. Control how much is used– he aims to dominate me. To him, I'm just a piece of meat. Disposable flesh used to maintain his elusive identity. Good thing I belong to me.
Relieved I center me.

**– Serina Jamison**

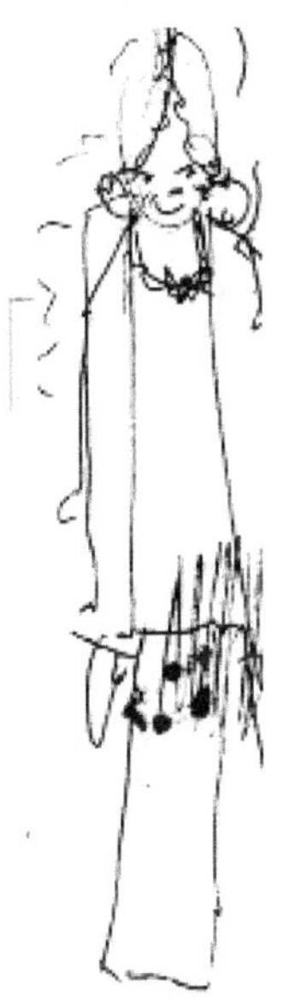

–Emma Travitz

**Flesh**

There is a lot that is carried within flesh
        scars as *memories*
        touch as *memories*
And while some welcome the change to flesh
others recoil
Because they know how lasting and permanent
That change to flesh can be

**– Amara M. Aguilera**

I didn't smoke my ghost weed
          so I can't flesh out many ideas
I wander sober
          the snow melts on my face
Inspiration deregulation
          static stagnation
Get off my ass and contemplate
Flesh of my flesh, blood of my fate
A pile of skin and bones
                    that can't relate
to the mounds of concrete
          stuck in one place
While I'm all over
          everywhere circulate

**– Jacob McElrone**

When I think about it,
Specifically yours…
Downy and Speckled. All the
Way warm, at all times.
I have to stop myself most
days from digging my four fingers
deep under your Ribcage.
It's still too much for me
when you Just get out of
the Shower, Warmer still,
Beads of Moisture on your
Strawberry flesh. One day
I'll take A NIBBLE.

**–Annabella**

**Blank**
      the clean slate we all long for.
None of the mistakes and all of the
possibility still ahead.
      But who wants to be a dumb baby?

**– Erin Caffrey**

**Elbows**

When you force yourself away from that which you cannot resist, what is left?

It's the early days. You are standing next to each other under a streetlamp. Your elbows touch, the exact same skin temperature. Something inside you, something with edges you normally can't feel, is alive and awake and curious, reaching for that person next to you.

It is almost assuredly your selfish, wishful thinking, but you know Biblically, anciently, humanly, that their soul must be moving the same way. You know that nobody in time nor space has stood where the two of you stand now, illuminated form above just so, feeling this exact intersection of temperature and humidity and elbows and souls.

And then, joy upon joy, this newly alive part of you is growing. It was newly born and uncertain, but with eye contact, its childhood begins. Its adolescence blossoms with that kiss, that first kiss that feels like a time-lapse video of a candle burning all the way down in seconds. Your eyelashes trade cheeks to brush, the hinge of your jaw aches for its turn with that mouth. The best, the best dawn of adulthood you can imagine; you make love in the night air and the sounds except for the movement of the river don't matter.

This maturation of your soul, just in time for summer. It couldn't be more perfect. Except– you are alone. "I don't feel that way… about you."

Immediately, those edges curl. Such a denial demands that something give. You command yourself to conform to reality, forget that deep knowledge of which you were sure. The weeks wear on, and you don't just lose that free and rapturous part of yourself. You lose your posture, your aura, your eye contact.

At night, away from this person, you ruminate to sand yourself down. Maybe a little less will finally be an acceptable shape. "Be reasonable," you tell yourself.

It feels impossible that this person, who added a whole new part to you, renders you just a little bit less every day. After a while, you ruminate laying next to them too. Though you get smaller, it never gets easier.

Is it enough to mean that you were honest this time when you said you never felt this way before?

You shut it down, you turn it away. You deny yourself their elbow, the streetlamp, the most unique weather conditions of late unique weather conditions of late spring on the most important night in the history of time.

So what is left?

**–Janae Mancheski**

What do you know about
aching arms gathering words
in groups of three?
Did you hear me when I
told you I don't care to remember
the things we write on walls or
the directions the arrows tell us to go?

If my hip is strong enough to
carry all the thoughts in my pocket
when the choices are down to none
My pride won't be strong enough to
notice the breath that will keep my mind
blank.

**– Shana Lucas**

**– Jack Leverenz**

# Refuse

Refuse to pay
for the sheertex
Just ate shit
in my $6.99
Walgreens tights
Bloody knee
No runs
              — ??

# REFUSE

I don't often refuse.
In fact, I have a hard time
Ever refusing.

I can't say no in the face of a
Decision.

In the face of him coming over,
I ask myself if I want this.
It would be easier to refuse.

He's drunk.
We both know this is a bad idea.
I encourage.

I've always encouraged.
Constantly disappointed.
Why don't I refuse?
Embarrassed again
I don't often refuse.
↓
I wish I refuse your advance.

**– Natasha Bivins**

**i refuse! (a princess manifesto)**

i refuse to stop shit
posting on my twitter
for i must share
w/ my people!!!

i refuse to stop
wearing silly little bows
in my hair!

i refuse to ignore little
luxuries
like:      ●GIRLS VAPING
          ●IGNORING HW
          ●FORGETTING THINGS
           ON PURPOSE

But most of all
(DEAR READER, WHEN YOU
READ THE NEXT LINES,
PLEASE YELL!)
I REFUSE TO LIVE A
LIFE I DO NOT DESERVE!!

      – E. T.

I refuse to buy gas for less than ten dollars per gallon. I compare premium gas to an amazon prime subscription. If I didn't owe the bank of chase a substantial amount already, I would buy more gasoline. I tell my financial advisor that I've invested in crude oil (bought more gas). Don't get me wrong, I refuse to buy a hummer. I actually own three electric cars, but they won't take premium gas.

**– Barry Quinnies**

**REFUSE**

I refuse to write anything substantial that will be read out loud.
Sorry! I'm a scared princess!
The pea under my 10,000 mattresses is second-hand embarrassment-
But Adeline says it hurts her feelings
So I'm working on it ♥
20203= vulnerable Fifi!!!

**–Fiona Bingley**

# FLAT

## Air Bags

I fell flat on my ass
cracked my tailbone, I swear,
heard my father scold me
on the way down

"Those damn shoes,
I told you 'throw them out', and
now you've gone and
fucked yourself."

Curled myself into
a ball to save
the laptop in my backpack
Hit the rock salt before
the pavement. Rung my

Ribcage like a bell
Folded over. Sat still.
Saw the blood on my palm.

But my Fat Ass saved my spine,
and I walked home
to soak in the tub.

**– Lily Lalios**

## FLAT

-Buongiorno, Nona! Say, tell me, how do they make this gosh darn RC cola taste so good?

-Well, that's a great story! Abbondanza! His name was Ricardo Cappolacola and he invented that beverage you're sipping. Ricardo Cappolaocola was a complicated man. Grew up in Hamden, Connecticut, studied philosophy, and had a sick mullet. But he was discontent, that Ricardo Cappolacola, and he wanted a change in his life. He managed a shoe shop and discovered that a small amount of shoe polish would react to the iodine in his Hamden, Connecticut municipal drinking water. The shoe polish would make the water sparkle, bubble, fizzle, froth!

It was amazing! He bottled the liquid, sold it for a half pence, and it quickly caught on! Pretty soon everyone was drinking Ricardo Cappolacola's invention. After a few weeks, the whole town of Hamden, Connecticut got violently ill from drinking diluted shoe polish. They chased Ricardo Cappolacola out of town!

Once he was gone, some other guy named Craig made RC cola.

-What the fuck, Nona? That story kinda sucked.

-You didn't like it?

-No. It really fell flat.

**– Tim Knapp**

**Tip Your Bartenders**

When I've toiled all day, and can't feel my back
When the boss cracks his whip, and won't give me no slack
I'll go tap on the bar, and sit where I sat
"Serve me a beer, and don't serve that shit flat."

He served me my drink, set it down with a tap
thumbed his nose with a smirk, caught my eye with a snap
"Enjoy your damn drink," his voice gave me regret
"Savor the foam, man, it's the last head you'll get."

**– Cody Burt**

# SQUARE

## Dog Food

My studio apartment was like 18 square feet
I paced back and forth talking on the phone
and got dizzy. My dog took up more space
than me. His bag of dog food was bigger
than my refrigerator. I worked 3 ½ jobs to
afford his grain-free dog food. Two were
at coffee shops. One was in a factory.
The half was this phone repair shop that
I showed up to when they called me
frantically asking me to come in and
fix iPad screens which I didn't
know how to do. The iPad is a
rectangle. The screen is a square.

You gotta line it up just right.
When I got home from work my dog
was all on edge. "What's wrong
Blair?" I asked him. His name was
Blair. He escorted me outside, into the
backyard, into the woods, through someone else's
yard, through a soccer field behind an elementary
school, and up a hill. "Bark! Bark!" he said.
"Bark!" I dug where he pointed.

Clawed and clawed with my human nails,
scratched at dirt, and hit something solid.
A briefcase. I unlatched it. It was full
of cash. Hundreds. Thousands. Millions? Maybe.
"Thanks for the dog food," said Blair. "Now we're square."

— **Tim Knapp**

## Square

It's just a shape
or the root of all my problems
math was never my strong suit
"you can't fit one in a round hole"
at least that's what my grandfather said

the word chosen by my ex when she said we
were no longer equals
there was a lack of intimacy

in a room of circles I was the only goddamn square
I still am
Only now, I've moved to a different room.

**–Gorman**

<u>Window Pain</u>

This square is transparent
From this side I feel so uncarin'.
I'm still alive 'cause this fire inside
But how can they survive with that
wind outside?

This square is transparent.
I'm sure to them I seem so despairing
How will I survive with this cold
outside?
I could die tonight if the wind
won't subside.

**–Shelton**

# RISK

## Risk

- the weight of eye contact
- lipstick
- too-big shoes (much too large)
- "non slip" boots
- hot on the windowsill
- indoor plumbing
- See You Next Tuesday
- foggy windows
- #girlswhosmokevapes
- internal temperature
- open flames
- stacked glasses
- the given; the absence of choice; we have to be alive
- restringing a violin
- decibels (many)
- blood that refuses to move
- the business
- wrong paper
- the brain, not yet developed
- the brain, calcified
- FERMENTATION
- poorly made fonts
- fraudulent holes
- forgetting to put it in the dryer
- tempo
- aliens
- hooligans
- (give a man a pen)
- loose balloons
- mold
- big jump
- the noise show
- analogue bodies:
- salt & electricity

**– Ira George**

## Fear

Reward-
World Domination
Deal.
Done.
Buy sell her
sell self to self
over and over
me/you
we are the world
didn't you hear?
soup covers the world, not paint
>insert reference about universal liquid
proof of satisfaction guaranteed
grenade motherfucker
how to get free
tithing on your porn money
Security
Insurance is a scam
No one knows how to experiment anymore
taste of rejection never hurt nobody
total wild west story
that's Rhinestone neon cowgirl to you good sir, er, whatever
someone has to die eventually, right?
or at least take a break for a while

**– Rielly Heintz**

# RISK

What is there to say about risk?
**This** is risky






**– Natasha Bivins**

# Fail

## Poor Noah

You are ten years old. You are supposed to grade the test of the smartest kid in class. You want to be funny. You think, "He won't get that many answers wrong." So you write FAIL when he gets an answer wrong. It's a good joke, for one or two answers. But for poor Noah, this is a (rare) very bad test. Soon, his entire paper was covered in the word FAIL, in all caps, just like that. You're not exactly one to let a bit die. Being the smartest kid in class, maybe he needed a hit on his self esteem. But 16 years later, I want Noah to know that he's not a failure.

**– Janae Mancheski**

## The Contented

I am content to fail.
Not out of self-contempt,
or a "weak-willed fatalism"
as the famous lover of fate
once worded it–
He was my favorite,
And though he never shirked it,
some say he was a failure.
But anyway–
I am content to fail.
Like Jack and Jill
And Sisyphus still
Never, ever overcoming the hill.
It is my will;
I am content to fail.
What a burden it is to fill that pail!
When we know in the end, the water goes stale.
So come on man,
Roll your boulder with me
Along the brass rail
Just take it easy
And be with me–
I am content to fail.

**– Sarah Pope**

Having failed to catch the bus (the last of the night), my way home would be cold and tiring. Grappling against the wind, I carried forward. By passing through the icy field, I would cut 5 minutes from my journey. The glow of the streetlights grow dim. I should not have stopped to watch that opossum. It wasn't really an opossum anyway. More of a plastic bag.

**– Ben**

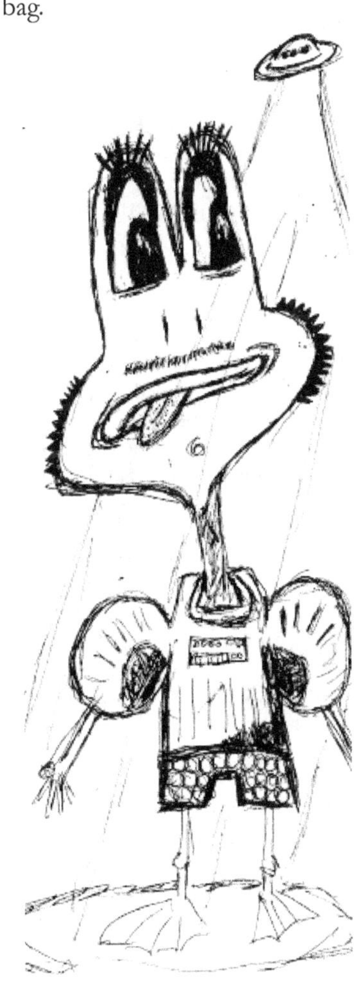

**Fail**

3:12 PM.
Tuesday.
In February.
Last week it snowed. Most of it is gone now, but it's still cold as balls.
Doesn't matter too much. It's only a single block away.
I'll survive.
There's no "ding" as I enter. Was there ever a ding? I wouldn't know until later
A clerk looks at me as I enter. I look back meekly.
I look away and quickly enter the first aisle I see. I think the clerk is still staring but I don't appease them.
I don't know what I'm looking for exactly, but I'm not leaving with nothing.
Looking.
Nah.
Looking?
Nope
Corner after corner after corner.
And I realize I'll have to settle eventually. I don't even care what at this point.
I mean I don't care a lot. Mom only sent me thirty dollars.
I reach out to the shiniest thing I see.
RED VELVET Bailey's Irish Cream™ . The **only** one **left.**
This will do.
The clerk turns from her phone to  the red bottle.
I raise my ID with a sweaty hand. In my other hand are my renewed paperwork.
He stares at it for a good while. I wonder if he's ever seen someone from Minnesota before.
He hands it back. I give him my mom's cash and I leave. I wonder if he was still looking as I left.
Back in the cold, I take a single step.
Oh NO.
Ice. The bottle wobbles out of the bag. I fail to catch it.
RED Velvet Bailey's Irish Cream™ everywhere. And now all I have are red stained hands
and red stained pants

**–Connor Thissen**

# Cast

## Cast

I went to Ireland to see my friend and I didn't see my friend until the last day when I was so sleep deprived and nauseated from the dark beer and the whiskey and the blood pudding which is congealed blood and oats sometimes and when I saw my friend we drank dark beer and whiskey and strong tea and I took a train to the bus to the airport, slept on the floor, everyone around me was snoring and shivering and fucking and I got on the plane to sleep and sat between these chatty lads, talked forever, asked me questions about Chicago, we cheersed Bud Light, they said they were from Belfast.

We met in the school play he invited me fishing with his uncle we didn't catch anything his uncle made crass jokes we ignored them the play was Cats and we both played one of the cats I couldn't sing but nobody could we kept in touch through college he moved to Ireland after and nobody believed that we were in Cats nobody believed that all the other actors came with us to the uncle's cabin when the uncle wasn't there we drank fireball we drank Bud Lite Lime we put our feet in the lake we didn't catch anything we all got trashed.

I talk to him on WhatsApp it's big there in Ireland he told me about a job I could get in Cork organizing spreadsheets and it wouldn't be fun in America but I applied to do it in Ireland and I bombed the zoom interview forgot everything every job I ever had forgot my own name asked how much I'd get paid and they didn't like that I didn't get the job I'm still in America it's okay it's all in the past.

When we got to O'Hare we drank like three or eight more eleven dollar Bud Lites we took the Blue Line we went to bars Chicago liked their accents but didn't like mine I tried a fake one I said lad a lot and a lotta lads don't like that they don't like that they didn't like me I dodged a punch I swear threw a couple of my own I swear everyone was swinging everyone was Irish I woke up in a cast.

– Tim Knapp

**CAST**

This guy has literally kept the same reading list, book list, suit and tie for the last 20 years, man. His high school students are still rolling their eyes at Romeo. "But why didn't they just run away together," they ask every year since 1995. Mr. Baker loves the dust and Comic Sans is his baby.

Sammy Simpson, Mrs. S, Maine South alumni and cracks jokes like a sailor. Can't help but gossip with the star quarterback about his latest hook-up. Most teachers pass Mrs. S in the hallway as she leans against the lockers, talking to Johnny Football. Mrs. S, never left high school.

The Irish Lady with the big red curly hair brought in a small plastic sword today, dagger? Macbeth. And you could hear her from across the room. The door slammer... or actually the one you slam the door on because you can hear even her lips smack and the head thrown back laugh. Loves to read.

Mr. J, the department head loves to head things loves to head this cast loves to tell the English teachers they are changing lives and changing worlds. A day in the life. Loves to head book clubs.

**– Alex Gambacorta**

"How long do I need to have this on?" he whined impatiently, tugging at his mother's sleeve.

"Just two more weeks," she said, not looking up from her computer screen.

He plopped down under her desk, dragging the neon green cast across the bumpy poster, past cords and an outlet. The fiberglass made a pleasant sound as it strummed the ridges and valleys of the wall, so he tried going faster. "Michael, please stop fidgeting, I'm still at work," his mother scolded.

The cast dropped onto the carpet with a muffled thud. It was a soft, warm thud, that sounded like it came from a stretched leather hand drum. Closing his eyes, Michael imagined he sat on a street corner, playing the drum for spare pocket change. The beat grew louder, stronger, and a crowd started to gather in the street. "What's your name?" an older gentleman inquired, "You're the best drummer I've ever heard! What's your name?"

"--Michael!" His mother's shrill voice vanquished the old man.

"Please be quiet or go somewhere else!"

"But Dave's in the other room!"

"He won't hurt you anymore, your father talked to him."

"You always say that."

She sighed. "You know he can't help it."

Michael laid down on his back and studied the underbelly of the desk. He flung his arm up.

"But I'm the one that has to wear this thing."

She paused, not sure what to say.

"Life isn't fair."

**– Vivian Coenen**

## By Order of the King

A coin dedicated to a long day's labor slapped against the ancient bar-top with a thunk. Clasping the thing was a meat-hook of a hand, fingers thick and calloused, with hair cascading into a forearm rippled with muscle. Or rather, ropes of muscle. The barkeep knew this man well, often the only patron to visit in the time between lunch and dinner. A blacksmith worked the hours he chose and not a soul would complain about the only smith within a day's travel.

"Been working Jameson's plough hitch?"

"Nah." The giant arm picked up the coin again and began tapping it idly. "'Nother order came in that can't be delayed."

The barkeep turned from pouring the smith's drink and was surprised to see a frown on the man's face. Placing the drink down, he leaned back and studied his patron. The smith was a smart man to be sure, but not one for melancholy or concern. After a moment, the smith placed the coin back on the bar, though gingerly this time. Moving to the bar, the barkeep lifted the coin with some surprise.

"What's this?" he asked while giving the thing a closer look. "I've never seen one like it."

"Payment for the new request." The smith shut his downcast eyes. "It's enough to buy half this place."

"What in God's name?" The barkeep placed the coin back on the counter. "Who could possibly pay with this? What did they buy?"

"My time."

"That's not much of an answer."

The hulking smith sat in silence for a long moment. Thick tension smothered the room as the barkeep waited for some explanation.

"That plough's the only one Jameson's got, isn't it?"

"Yes."

"Thought so." The smith picked up the coin and replaced it with one that paid for his untouched drink before rising from his seat.

"When he comes in, can you tell him to come by and pick up his hitch? He'll need to take it out of town."

"Of course! But… where are you going?"

"Got to get to work casting some iron."

**– Cody Burt**

# Turn (Egg)

## Archetypal Struggles

I walk down the dark street, terrified. I can feel his presence around every turn. I catch glimpses of him in the corners of my vision. He is getting closer. I cannot seem to ever escape him. I run down a back alley, there he is behind me. I am trapped.
"It's okay now," a deep voice calls out. I turn to face him. It's him, it's Mr. Egg, I think to myself. His deep blue eyes, his soothing face, his strong veiny thighs, the man from my nightmares I would recognize anywhere.
"It's all over now. No need to worry." Mr. Egg picks me up. He kisses my forehead. It reminds me of home, a feeling I haven't felt since I was a child. A single tear rolls down my cheek. He cracks me, he fries me on a hot pan, and serves me on a piece of rye toast…
Yolk still running.
Fin.

**– Dr. Michael Heck, Sr.**

"Monsieur Egg?" a silky baritone spoke softly. The pilot's blue eyes
fluttered open and slowly took focus on his captor. "You must understand we've put an end to your schemes," the captor went on.
"Oui," the downed pilot said in a half-whisper, no looking deeply
into the eyes opposite him, "but you fail to understand your own
game, my friend." The man facing him stood up abruptly and flipped
switch after switch. Pale lights flooded a factory floor, cleared in the
center save the hunched, once-proud figure of France's most feared
fighter pilot. He dropped his head between his shoulders, reciting the
downed fighter's mind-melt.
The captor whispered to his captive once more. "Pray your people
can forgive your sins." He held a microphone, which he switched on
and spoke into, gesturing to the crowd gathered around Egg. "This,
you poor people, is your supposed hero, who you trusted to protect
your skies. Now look at him, and hear his great evil which he has
failed to let you all know: he drinks beer on ice, he smokes Camel
Crushes and ACTUALLY crushes them, and I regret to tell you, de-
spite what his Instagram says, he does NOT have big things coming
soon."

**– Riley Marks**

I was driving home from the grocery store, just one street away. The
light turned green, but I forgot, it wasn't my right-of-way. I smelled
fresh exhaust, my foot sank down to those pretty old floorboards.
Then bang, crash, crunch. I fade to black in my Honda Accord.
When I woke I saw the prettiest eyes a man could see. For it was he,
Mr. Egg man, whose left turn it had happened to be.

**– Bridger Flory**

# FACE

**Diary of an astrophysicist with a child in Pre-K**

Dear Diary,
You would not believe what my child brought home today. She drew
a picture of our house, which is fine. But, she put a picture of the
sun in the corner. With little triangles for rays! She even colored it
yellow and orange (yellow I can understand– some people call it a
"yellow dwarf" but in actuality, it is white).

But worst of all, she drew the sun with a smiley face and
sunglasses on it. I can't believe this. My life's work, rendered a com-
plete absurdity by my own progeny. I have clearly failed, as a mother,
to teach her anything of value.

It's like she doesn't even know that one day the sun will
expand and engulf the Earth, or that it's made of helium and hy-
drogen. It's like she's not even thinking of the low-frequency hum
NASA has recorded of the ball of gas processing itself. No, it's not
a magnificent celestial body. Now, it's just a crayon-yellow circle with
a lopsided expression. It's even less sophisticated than the ancients
worshiping the sun as a a god and personifying it.

Honestly, I expected more. I'll have to rethink her fifth birthday present.

**– Janae Mancheski**

## Disco Lights

I wonder at the glitter coating your cheeks, rosy and glimmering under disco light. We've been swaying for hours to pounding 808s and cascading rhythm beats. Is it the vodka soda in my glass or the revelation of endless nights?

We'd sit under the stars. "I wish we could stay here forever," you said, counting until sunrise bled across the sky.

I see constellations in your eyes tonight; uncountable as ever. Pulling at your waist, holding you tight. "We'll dance," I say, "until the morning light."

And dance we do, always keeping pace. Pushing a lock of hair behind your ear, I whisper "Let me look at you and be lost in your starry face."

**– Cody Burt**

**Saving Face**

Sam's face stung with little beads of frozen rain that struck her. She scuttled to her girlfriend Fiona's apartment with a six pack of beer hanging from her fingers. At least the beer would be cold.

She felt a buzz in her left pocket and knew it was Fiona asking where the fuck she was, and that it was going to be a shit birthday with no booze. Sam let her feet carry her forward, two more blocks and she'd be there, no need to reply.

As she reached the old oak tree outside Fiona's apartment Sam was so excited to get inside, she didn't see the equally upset figure coming from the opposite street. Sam flung open the front door of the apartment complex and struck the stranger in the face.

"Oh my god, I'm so sorry!" Sam gasped as the stranger held his eye.

"Motherf—" Sam didn't hear the last half as she rushed up the staircase. In the greenhouse heat of the apartment, Sam presented the beer to Fiona and took off the ruined coat she came in.

"I'm so sorry I'm late," she said, giving Fiona a quick peck on the cheek. "I was anxious, I wanted to make a good first impression."

"It's okay," Fiona said, "My dad texted, he's just getting here now."

**– Lily Lalios**

**– Clemens**

# STONE(D)

It was well past time when we started shooting people at the altar.
Death as a remedy was typically relegated to lands
where hippos and baboons terrorized tourists
But then we took to aiming at trees as
they whispered on the playgrounds or turned themselves
into books and benches.
I tried to pick up arms but I have no hands
So I choose to run instead.
As soon as the firestorms tore through the sky
I gathered the last of my peace
And left this land, never looking back
lest I turn into salt or stone.

**– Shana Lucas**

## Chained to Hades

I'm standing atop a great mount. One which exhausted my body, sapping strength from every fiber. Effort unseen in my time or any to follow. No man, woman, god, or devil had conquered the pinnacle in my fashion. And I, as should be recorded in the annals of history, defeated this trial THRICE.

I spoke to my lord that he could not have me as a vassal. I am a King. A lord, in my own time, over a great people. Twice I evaded him. Twice, strikes at my station could not find purchase. I stand by my pride, rightfully earned, but I can admit imperfection. The final attempt had me and finally I have overcome my punishment. An insecure punishment for my pride and clever mind.

Fool of a lord he is, though; tasking me with a feat of strength. This great stone would crush any soul lesser than my own, and yet I stand here before it, triumphant. My success cannot be denied. I must take care stepping around the boulder, however. If not for a clumsy step each of the other times, I'd be released from these chains. Simply step around this stone and I may return from my mountain prison, renewed. My people await in trembling anticipation for their absent King: Sisyphus!

**– Cody Burt**

**A True Story:**

Saint Stephen is… kind of a dick, if you ask me. For one, he flaunted
his knowledge of Greek in front of everyone in Jerusalem, pre-
tending he couldn't understand their language. He pretended to care
about old sick widows just to make Hebrews feel bad. Get a load of
this— he was an evangelist, which means he basically ran around asking people for money and telling them to stop buttfucking.
Like most people completely subsumed in religion and their own
egos, he defended himself in court. You know the type— the only guy
around who speaks fluent Greek, helping old ladies across the street,
burning rainbow flags. Obviously, he lost the case.
Guess what happened then? The townspeople dragged him out to
the wilderness and started throwing shit at him. There's not exactly
a lot of flora around Jerusalem, so eventually they started throwing
rocks. Stephen curled up in a ball and started crying like a little snob-
by baby. He actually died of embarrassment, not stoning.
I've always preferred Francis of Assisi, to be honest.

    **– Janae Mancheski**

## Stoned on a Full Moon Eclipse

For legal purposes, this is a joke.
If I look paranoid, don't pry or poke.
I have to confess, I've taken a toke.
An ironic gag for you humorous folk

Legally speaking, I'm not really *wink* stoned
I've committed no act that the law won't condone
My eyes are just like that, don't take that tone.
You try writing high, man, throw me a bone.

**–Lily Lalios**

It was well past 2am as I turned in to the driveway; a large, white quarry stone was illuminated in the headlights. I made sure to maneuvre the car carefully, as that quarry stone was the marker where a drainage ditch ran through. I pulled up to the garage and turned off the headlights, as not to disturb the rest of the sleepy subdivision. I turned up the Cat Stevens song on the radio, reached into the secret panel of the driver's side door, and plucked out a pipe, already partially packed with Racine's finest green. I cracked the window, sparked, and puffed. "♪ But tell me; where do the children play? ♪" I remembered playing on that big quarry stone as a kid; it brought me back to a simpler time, and made me wonder how I got here. Now…
Suddenly the garage door began to open, and the light from inside slowly poured out onto the driveway in front of me. A slender silhouette stood there still, staring at me. I stashed the pipe quickly as my father approached the car.
"Whatcha doin.?" he asked.
"Oh, just listening to music."
"Well, your muffler is pretty loud. Maybe turn the car off."
"Oh shit. Sorry. Sure," I blushed.
"Okay. Don't stay up too late."
"I won't. Goodnight."
"Goodnight!" he said, and as he walked away, he turned back and asked: "Do you smell a skunk?"

**– Nick Westfahl**

So, I went to my Ma's funeral a few days ago, real cool-like. Pop was there, crying into his handkerchief, a real woe-is-me type, sputtering away like his periwinkle Buick. Anyway, I was late to the damn thing because the tire I stole to replace my flat tire was flat itself and I didn't even notice, being stoned myself. My grandma was holding Ma's obituary, having called the police to ask if they found the bastard that killed her. This made me nervous, since I'm the one that did it. I know, I know! But now you see why I had to be real cool about it. Why did I kill her? She was rude to me one time back in '93, and I had to do it. Sure, it took me 30 years but you can't rush it. One year was too hot, the next too cold or rainy. It was a mess! Probably gonna have to ride in a van out west and then live in said van and play the ukelele or something stupid like that. Can you believe my luck?

**–Dally Du Mez**

2COOL²

# LIFT

## The Lottery

"Hey, I need a lift." Emmett leans against my doorframe, his feet carefully positioned to be outside of my room. Childhood arguments of "GET OUT OF MY ROOM" "I'M NOT IN YOUR ROOM!" echo around him.

"Can't you drive?" I look over from my laptop screen. I'm supposed to be writing an essay on the connection of weasels to vampiric folklore. I wrote the title and then god distracted playing Cool Math Games and reliving middle school days. I'm always surprised by how Emmett's fluffled hair almost touches the top of the doorframe. There used to be a time when he was smaller than me, when I could lift him over my shoulder and shove him in a closet long enough to run back to my room and block the door.

"My car's in the shop," he says.

"Oh yeah, you totaled it."

"Not my fault." His pitch rises defensively.

"Didn't you drive into a stoplight?"

"Can you please just give me a ride?"

"Where?"

"The gym."

"It's four in the morning."

"So? I need the gains."

"Fine, whatever."

In the car he pulls out his phone.

"So why'd you run into a stoplight?" I ask.

He huffs. "I was distracted."

"By what?"

"None of your business."

"You suck."

"You swallow." He sticks his tongue out. I do the same. He slouches in his seat and sighs. "I think I'm gay," he says.

I brake so hard, he smashes into the dashboard. "I'm sorry, what?"

"What?" he asks, "You homophobic, Miss Liberal?"

"Excuse me? I'm just surprised, Mr. Vaping-makes-you-gay. Did you vape?"

"No. I just think I might be gay."

"Why?"

"I kissed a guy. That's why I ran into the stoplight."

"Huh."

"That's it? Huh?"

"What else do you want me to say?"

"I don't know, something nice."

"You're gay, not winning the lottery."

"I just thought you'd have more of a reaction."

"Emmett, I already knew you were gay. You're better at eyeliner than me."

He stares at the ceiling. "Thanks for the lift."

"Yeah, no problem."

**– Odi Welter**

I adjust my vest. Stupid thing is constricting my chest. The pinstripes
might as well be cell bars over my lungs. The air is so heavy with
smoke, I watch it curl in on itself before being dragged into some
babe's mouth. Her long cigarette hangs loosely from her fingers, ash
dropping down and burning the velvet couch beneath her. Her man
has his arm snugly wrapped around her. She laughs, pressing into his
side. Beautiful as a dove she is with her hair laminated in waves. My
eyes drag up and down her form before meeting the gaze of her fella.
I realize I need air, desperately. I struggle through the maze of the
club. Left and right, following the walls until I find the door. Pulled
up right next to the door is a shiny new Model T with the doll of the
club stretched out across the seats. Standing, leaning against the car's
door is her male counterpart. His eyes meet mine once again as he
opens his mouth for the first time of the night, "Need a lift, friend?"

**– Madelyn Schneider**

**Find Your Dream Job Today!**

"Must be able to lift up to 50 pounds daily"
That makes no goddamn sense. Why would a tech support position
EVER lift 50 pounds? Whoever writes these job descriptions is on
the kinda shit I'd kill for. I have to pay 20 for a gram of the driest shit
you've seen in your life while a divorced middle-manager flies high on
some Vogue-ass designer shit, just to punch in.

Fuck it.
I'm just gonna jump off a cliff.

The whole thing, doing bullshit work, earning bullshit wages, living in
bullshit apartments with bullshit landlords.
All of it can burn. I hate it.
Why can't I just grab the boat, hop on a lake, throw back a couple
beers, and yank on a line in some sunlight?
Every day I'm forced to fight for my life. All to live a way that makes
me want to die.
Fuck.

**– Cody Burt**

# CHIP

## Over Pour

I'll chip my tooth on you
Sharp as a rocks glass

Cut my tongue and watch
The blood drip down my chin

You make me taste like
a fine vintage. Barrel

oaked and full bodied
with notes of leather

and fresh cut grass.

**– Lily Lalios**

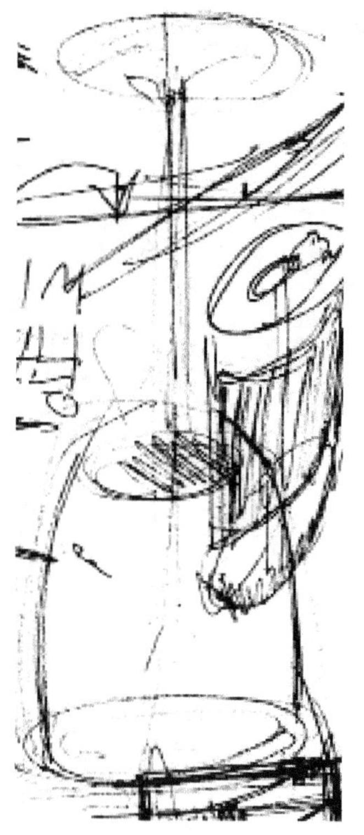

**Chip**

He greatly cherished the sound of bones cracking; it was the very reason for his profession. The bones would be given to him nicely packaged and whole, and all he had to do was cut them free—this was part of the fun, retrieving the bones. Carving them out from their quivering trimmings, wrapping his fingers around such firm and certain comforts. It was warm and messy, which he liked, and there was no measure to the joy he felt as everything but the bones fell away. Their skin was ribbons, their muscles in origami folds, and the hearts they clung to so dearly were crushed like grapes for wine.

He preferred the skulls above all else. A scalpel slid so cleanly across the forehead, so delicate. Skulls were so easy to crack, and made the most satisfying sound. Tap-tap with his mallet, and they would fracture as though as thin as a butterfly's wing.

The problem was the sight of the break. It was too imperfect, an undeserving blemish on the surface of such precious bone, and so he would find himself tapping more, hammering, even throwing his entire arm into splitting the skull into tiny chips that could be puffed away with a breath. Then the sight of perfect bone was gone, and he would go to seek it out again. Each time, however, he kept a new chip of skull in his pocket.

**–Lily Kreitz**

## The Art Below the Surface

Chip into my rough exterior,
carve me from marble,
and chisel your tip into my essence

Underneath, you may discover
striations amber and amethyst
burned into my skin

I want you to find me
at the junctions of love and pressure
seek me
where the art meets the artist

Explore me,
until the sun peeks over the horizon
and you wipe the sweat from your brow,
evidence of the night's labor

**– Dally Du Mez**

# MORE

## Lincoln Park, W Glendale Avenue

It's not enough for him to stand ten feet away from me in his uni-
form,
cracking a wolfish smile.

No, he edges closer, more teeth showing
I can see the black and white hairs making up his gray beard
He's five feet away now.

He shows me a picture of his daughter, older than me
and his grandchild.

He doesn't believe me when I say I'm twenty-three
(I'm not)

I step back, toward the trees, away from home.
"Come on now, I don't bite," he says.
But he looks like he grabs, tackles, stalks.

An excuse, an excuse, my kingdom for an excuse.

I finally wave goodbye, Midwest friendly,
and stride eastward as he drives off
in the county's truck,
which I've paid for in taxes.

All I wanted was to bring my dog to the park.
Nothing more.

      **–Janae Mancheski**

**More**

Yes, please.

   –**Justyn**

**Looks Like We've Got a Gusher**

I like to read
I like to write
Destiny's Child wanted more
Spotlight disco dancing
Creature of fire
Gets burned
Lesson learned for the
Sharp dressers
Loose lips
Improve ships
Get swabbing my deck
Poke man pokeCAN
Let me have
The **FULL** set
I explore wild and full on
Nature be damned
And I will overflow
Looks like we
Got a gusher
Ask permission to
Ask permission
Thanks for being you
Yes read and
Shine bright
EXCEED the some of
These parts
MORE MORE MORE
That's how we
LIKE IT

**– Adam Mckee**

**<<eXpresso>>**

He arrived an hour late,
dusty blue cuffs rolled up
over unearned nautical tattoos.
His thick, curly hair reigned in
by a plum beanie, he lugged
his tool kit onto the counter
next to the defunct espresso machine.

"What's wrong with it?" he asked,
tapping the brass-faced pressure gauge.
I huffed, only just disgusted,
"That's why I called you."
He didn't turn around, adjusting tubing,
confrontation not appealing to him.

He tapped and pinged, his greasy fingernails
along the casing. "How long is this going to take?"
I said. "More time than you have, I'm guessing," he
spat back.

"Fine," I said, "enough time to get my stuff.
Don't fuck up the shop while I'm gone."

He shivered at that, and turned
to ask for his keys, offering a freshly
pulled shot in exchange.

**– Lily Lalios**

## PAPERS Boy

Float not bound, recipe is whim
Look around and soak it in
Do you want MORE
Before we're ready to really begin?
Let's explore a film set in hypothetical skin
'Cause in the summer
            it might get loosy goosy
A strip mall reminder, stocking liquor part timer
Bend the rules
            of how they're moving
How's the upkeep, how ya doing?
            Ideology is exhausting
when keeping up appearances
            losing jobs running mouths
                        Talking about
I forgot my papyrus
            so lend me this paper
And I'll sit right beside it

**–Jacob McElrone**